Alice and Greta's Color Magic

by Steven J. Simmons

illustrated by Cyd Moore

ALFRED A. KNOPF NEW YORK

For Sara, thanks for inspiring A & G on the hill all those years ago, and for Tom and Sylvia, thanks for your friendship—S.J.S.

For Jay, who was born to sail through the clouds, and for his best co-pilot, Becky.
—C.M.

THIS IS A BORZOI BOOK PUBLISHED BY ALFRED A. KNOPF

Text copyright © 2001 by Steven J. Simmons
Illustrations copyright © 2001 by Cyd Moore

All rights reserved under International and Pan-American Copyright Conventions. Published in the United States of America by Alfred A. Knopf, a division of Random House, Inc., New York, and simultaneously in Canada by Random House of Canada Limited, Toronto. Distributed by Random House, Inc., New York.

KNOPF, BORZOI BOOKS, and the colophon are registered trademarks of Random House, Inc.

Library of Congress Cataloging-in-Publication Data
Simmons, Steven J., 1946–
Alice and Greta's color magic / by Steven J. Simmons ; illustrated by Cyd Moore. — 1st ed.
p. cm.
Summary: After Greta, a naughty witch, causes trouble by casting a spell that drains all color from the world, she must team up with Alice, a kind witch, to set things right.
ISBN 0-375-81245-8
[1. Witches—Fiction. 2. Magic—Fiction. 3. Color—Fiction.] I. Moore, Cyd, ill. II. Title.
PZ7.S59186 An 2001
[E]—dc21
00-065495

www.randomhouse.com/kids

Printed in the United States of America
September 2001

10 9 8 7 6 5 4 3 2 1
First Edition

It was a bright sunny morning, and a witch named Alice was teaching her pet butterfly, Grace, to fly in circles. She thought this trick might amuse small children. When Alice asked Grace if she was getting dizzy, Grace turned her wings a bright turquoise, which meant no. When Grace wanted to say yes, she turned her wings flaming pink.

Greta was another witch, very different from Alice. Greta preferred to use her magical powers to stir up trouble. She also had a pet—a purple snake named Ormond. She was busy that morning casting a spell that made Ormond tie himself in knots and stick out his tongue. Greta snickered, knowing this would scare small children.

When Greta got bored with Ormond, she thought about what new mischief she might cause. She was still angry at Alice for putting an end to one of her devious schemes by landing her in a puddle of bug juice. Greta kept a giant sparkling green emerald, which would glow and suggest diabolical spells when she rubbed it. She used it now. Soon a picture of Alice appeared in the emerald. She had turned into a bat and was hanging upside down. Greta laughed loudly and kept rubbing.

Next came a picture of Ormond popping Alice's favorite balloons with his tongue. Greta cackled with delight.

But she kept rubbing, and after a while the emerald showed Alice dressed in bright pink, Alice with her beautiful butterfly, Alice watering bright flowers, and Alice painting pretty pictures. Alice's love of colorful things inspired Greta to come up with a wonderfully wicked idea. "I'll make sure that pink goody two-shoes won't be able to enjoy her butterfly, flowers, and painting anymore!"

Greta waved her wand and chanted,

Roses are red and violets are blue,
These are the colors I hate
through and through!

The red and blue in Alice's favorite flowers vanished at once. The blue color of the sky, oceans, and blue jays, and the red color of fire engines, apples, and valentines—all things Alice loved—disappeared from the earth. The sapphire and ruby in Alice's only two rings lost their luster as their colors drained away. A robin Alice liked covered his dull chest in shame.

But Greta was far from done.
The next morning she cackled,

Orange, orange, now disappear,
You're a terrible color I do not want here!

Alice's orange balloons couldn't be seen, and her favorite morning drink, orange juice, looked like water. All she could see of her plastic pumpkin was the smiling face.

Later that afternoon Greta pointed her wand and chanted,

Abragoodbye to the color pink,
It's a color that really does stink!

Pink disappeared from Alice's clothing and from two other things she really liked: cotton candy and clouds at sunset. When Alice asked Grace if she was okay, Grace had no way of saying yes.

Pleased with the results of her nasty spells, Greta waved her wand all around and shouted,

Frog's gut and lizard's eye,
To every color I say goodbye!

All color in the land disappeared.

Just as soon as Greta had finished this chant, she looked around and realized she had gone too far. Where was her favorite color—yucky green? Where was the green of her hat and clothes? How could she use her precious green emerald?

She quickly yelled,

Green, green, yucky green,
Return right now to this awful scene!

The color green instantly reappeared, and Greta smiled. She was
happy again, but everyone else was still upset.

Greta's friend Tim, who was a troll, complained to her about losing the red color of his hair. He had loved his red hair.

Alice was fuming. Where were Grace's colors? Where were the magnificent colors of her roses, violets, lilacs, and lilies? Where was her hat's pink shine? Without color all these things were bland and boring. I *know* Greta is behind this, she thought.

A school art class had just finished painting pictures of their homes when Greta's spell struck. The children, who had been proud of their work at first, now had tears in their eyes. The only colored parts of their pictures were treetops, grass, a sweater, and a few green doors.

Two peacocks ran into the bushes, embarrassed by their drab feathers.

A chameleon that changed colors to hide itself from bigger animals became very confused and curled up in a ball.

A brother and sister watching a beautiful rainbow were upset to see all of its colors except green disappear.

And boys and girls everywhere were sad. Where were the colors of their special pajamas, their favorite toys, and their stuffed animals? How could they decide what clothing to put on in the morning? Where were the different colors of children's hair and eyes and faces? Without these differences every boy and girl looked the same, and the world was dull and uninteresting.

After a while even Greta got tired of just the color yucky green. She missed seeing the orange of her spiders and the purple of her snake, Ormond. She missed the red of Tim's hair. And she missed the colors of the shirts and sweaters and hats and socks and the different faces of the girls and boys she liked to bother. She became sad and shed a great big green tear.

Meanwhile, Alice had decided to teach Greta a lesson. She would return the missing colors to the world, but she would make Greta's favorite, yucky green, disappear. "Let's see how Greta likes *that!*" she said to herself. Alice snuck up on Greta and pointed her wand. Remembering the most important lesson at Witch School, the Brewmerang Principle, she whispered,

Whatever you chant, whatever you brew,
Sooner or later comes back to you!

The world was full of color again. Except for green. Once more, Greta's hat, clothes, emerald, and wand were colorless. First, she was shocked. Then she was angry. She quickly decided to repeat the chant that had worked before. Shaking her wand, Greta screamed,

Green, green, yucky green,
Return right now to this awful scene!

But the spell did not work this time. Neither Greta nor Alice could believe what happened. Instead of bringing back the color green, the spell mixed up all the colors.

Alice and Greta realized that their color magic had gotten out of hand.

Alice confronted Greta and said, "We need to work together and get this straightened out." Greta had to agree. They talked about the magic spells they had studied at Witch School and finally decided that one in particular might work. Together they chanted,

Sun, moon, stars, and sea,
Put all colors where they should be!

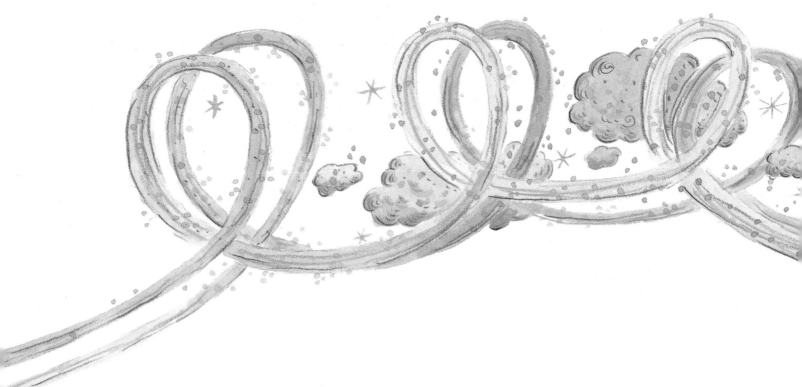

The spell worked! All the colors of the world returned to their normal places. Both witches were so delighted they did flying circles with their brooms. To make up for having started the mess, Greta dropped millions of colored lollipops on school playgrounds for children to enjoy. She sent a swarm of butterflies for Alice to play with. And she planted pretty flowers on the side of the mountain.

Grace was so happy she kept flashing her wings flaming pink.

Ormond looked in the mirror, relieved his purple had returned.

The peacocks came out from the bushes and proudly spread their feathers.

The chameleon crawled onto an orange leaf and grinned as he turned orange.

Tim beamed as he combed his red hair.

And smiles returned to the faces of children everywhere.

The world once again had the shades of difference that make it interesting, beautiful, and magical. Alice didn't know what to say. She had never known Greta to correct a mistake like this. Maybe she really *had* learned the Brewmerang Principle.

But as Alice flew over to thank Greta, she stopped. She saw Greta throw some bugs and lizards into her cauldron and heard her chant,

Time to brew, time to bubble,
Time to stir up nasty trouble!

Maybe Greta will never learn, thought Alice. But Alice thanked Greta anyway for helping bring back the magic of color. She then got on her broom and flew under a splendid rainbow into a bright blue sky.